# The Aviary

# The Aviary

poems by

*Miranda Pearson*

OOLICHAN BOOKS
LANTZVILLE, BRITISH COLUMBIA, CANADA
2006

**Library and Archives Canada Cataloguing in Publication**

Pearson, Miranda
    The aviary / Miranda Pearson.

Poems.
ISBN 0-88982-230-1

    I. Title.
PS8581.E388A95 2006    C811'.54    C2006-901951-7

We gratefully acknowledge the support of the Canada Council for the Arts for our publishing program.

Grateful acknowledgement is also made to the BC Arts Council for their financial support.

We acknowledge the financial support of the Government of Canada through the Book Publishing Industry Development Program for our publishing activities.

Published by
Oolichan Books
P.O. Box 10, Lantzville
British Columbia, Canada
V0R 2H0

Printed in Canada

For Adam Pearson-Currie

# Contents

## Fall Again

## Aerial

## The Empress

## Silver Collection

## Fall Again

*Raise the tent of shelter now,*
*though every thread is torn*

Leonard Cohen

## The Garden

In Spring's full zenith I go back, a shock
of green, all of it

fulfilled, the slow results
up and spread, the lilac tree

dripping its mauve flower, its
seduction. Your daughter's pale legs

sprout ghostly
through the French windows, this small plot

I coaxed from frost, worried over—
has grown on, fierce with loss.

Moss. Stacks of green plastic pots,
the watering can—relics

from afternoons in suburban nurseries,
and a red wheelbarrow still warm

    with the smell of earth—

# Proof

The rain woke me this morning. The drip drip of the cabin.
I am losing my grip. Everybody's breaking up
this long wet summer of shuffle-down and my knees
can't take it. The fronds here are like panting dogs.
A single iris, its defiant purple blade. I snap snap
pictures but turns out there's no film so:
a pretty garden with no proof.

I remember that awful woman at the party
her sushi-breath so close, so close
telling us of her *unwitnessed life*.
How we laughed about her afterwards.
You and I, did we make each other cruel?
Living alone now, our own obsessive little projects,
having shunned, having put Self-in-Dog-House,
having proved it, and proved it. Can cruelty stop now?

## Dog Walk, Kitsilano

Early morning, sheathed in rain
and the air is full of sound.

Navy blue clouds bloom
behind the houses, Isaac looks up

his tapered nose striped like a tiger-lily.
The grass he treads is wet

like the grass in my mother's garden,
best forgotten now. A pile of cut laurel twists,

crooked as recall, small
purple fists of rhododendron

swell but resist their showy release
into flower.

## On Christopher Lake

It's fall again, the ruby season.
My Greek-hipped canoe nudges
through reeds and I think about trust,
wonder if I'm beginning to catch on to it,
not turn so much
from human warmth. I think of the
small Buddha that sits by my sister's computer
to remind her, she said,
of "non-attachment".

I worried for her children then
but I guess she meant to "things". Her eyes,
always trained forward, green like bracken
or clear lake water, or our father's.
His brains too. I was the emotional one.
You couldn't be both.

Our mother said,
*you'll make someone a good wife one day.*
But now, an angular woman,
I'm often strange to myself. I have been
unable to replicate the family, only to take it apart
like an autistic child with a radio.

The lake is still. I'm in a mirror world—
the plumb of the boat's rope
in the tawny green water,
genius of float. My oar's pull
of symmetry and fabricated depth.

## Resuscitation

In the shallow end
the father dips his baby daughter,
his big palm supporting her head.
He's teaching her to swim
—and to trust, her slick throat
thrown back
like a lover's.

From the pool's edge I watch them
through my goggles' smokey lenses;
an outsider
trying to learn a language
awkward to my tongue.

> *I dive again and again*
> *through the cloudy water*
> *trying to reach the shape*
> *that lies down there like an*
> *old overcoat, or some great*
> *dark pelt—*

Somebody told me
it's possible to mend the past
through imagination, to breathe into it
a different life.

## The Aquarium

Cheery step-mother greets brickwall child,
his face glazed in front of the TV, its
ashy light. Last weekend they had all squashed
into her white car (seat-belts, kids!) and driven
through the rain-forest to the aquarium where she
claimed they were a *family* to get the cheaper rate.

The boy felt sure it was terribly wrong of her
to use that word, he would report it. They had
gazed silently at the blind spineless ballet of jellyfish,
the flowing shards of turquoise: tiny scars of light.
Then, at the octopus as it half-hid in the far
corner of its tank, its lewd orange clamps, its
reproachful, open eye.

# Skiing

The hotel lobby has a sculpture:
a tall jade oval with a hole in its centre.
You have gained weight since last time and
look older, more decadent, as we sit by the fire
on a maroon leather sofa, drinking dirty
martinis and vaguely considering an affair.

You have become someone who wants not to
think anymore, your scientist's brain
built up like a toppling high rise. You say
you like skiing because it's *good and mindless.*
I picture you gliding down the impassive mountain,
the soft hiss of your skis, statistics and theories
emptying out behind you. And this was a year

I turned away from poetry, as from a love
when it becomes too difficult, too close.
We choose instead snow-blindness, virgin white
like cocaine. Meetings in distant hotels, their
silent automatic doors, the knowing bowed head
of the doorman.

## I Want You

—so what if you don't believe me, how true is truth?
It slips and curdles, it loops apart. We're an idea, dear,
though in dreams you undress me. It takes forever, my red dress
with its long sleeves, a dozen pearl buttons at each wrist.
We're strange animals, aren't we, under all these clothes?
One body but two heads. And why is there always a mirror?
Lust slugs me, fogs me in. An infestation of ants
pouring from the wall, I'm distressed like leather, sick
of these dismal insights, *I, I, I,* sad heads lined up in the oven,
mouths gaping mid-confession like baby birds', your thin mouth
a closed slot I would make gurgle with coins.

## Galiano

        The sea: how easy
it is to get in
        but how tough it can be
to get out,
        the deceptive
razor's edge of barnacles.
        Waves
cutting us off, our sad waving from separate rocks
        and my hand
on the warm, blonde stone,
exploring the honey-comb.
        And later,
that grainy photograph in the craft-shop,
a woman's hand
on stone, her fingers long
and ring-less like mine.
        All day
there is talk of coincidence, everything
is heavy with metaphor
        when you are falling
in
        or out.

# Cherry

Of course, afterwards, we picture
the hanging tree, its classic stark silhouette.
Could she have noticed the harbour lights, or
the opening of the dawn?
Would the grass have been wet
on her bare feet as she walked to the tree?

It was four or five—no later. Would there
still have been stars? And did she
change her mind, wrap her legs
around the tree to save herself?
(We learn later from the coroner this is true).

We obsess over details,
the *hows* and the *wheres.* Just as
at a birth the chorus of voices focuses
on that moment only, in all its emergency

and not the years stretched out ahead
of caring for this child,
the ordinary, hard work of that—
the hard work, too, of being the child.

And still later, Brooke's tree—
being ordinary—flowered, along with all the others
in this best-spring-any-of-us-can-remember,
the branches heavy with white, reaching down
to the sea.

## Hornby

Warm driftwood and shale, so many
white coins running through our fingers

we watch the sky's evening dance—
improvised of course, as this is the

Gulf Islands and anything goes,
bright rags scatter violet while

right on cue the moon
makes its smooth

stage-y appearance (*it's behind you!*)
and the sea, hurried and patient both

in its introspect          *applause*
*applause*

## Here I Am, Lover

Why am I here?
It's blindingly obvious I prefer the embroidery of wild flowers
to these dark mountains that remind me
only of Scotland.

I should have seized the chance and stayed in the woods, watched
the silver birch unpeel, its flay
a crazy book, its tough, dry, weep.

Oh, the decoy of romance.
And you, waiting by the shore, *wanting* (always), your sex
a bright tongue, the horrible appetite of one who is too
hungry, your shirt damp from another night outdoors.

So, here I am, lover. With the stars.
And the starfish that cling on and on.
The arbutus is here, too,
and the crunching sea-shells.

You see the housework of tide everywhere,
the way it sweeps things up. Forgets.

Glance quizzically at the sun. Breathe        that deep smell of salt,
the sodden initiation of air.
I am meagre, like winter sunlight.

But feel that? The thump and sway of berth (ooh, shudder)
as the ferry, you know, *connects*. Only
see the dock's ragged black stockings,
hear the huff and shrug of sea, masculine, dogged. Its bellows
hardworking, obsessive.

I come back to you and lay at your feet
an empty bowl.
Poetry:
>                         bric-a-brac.
These small stitches,
this picking
and unpicking.

*Try*, will you, to repair longing. My heart
weighs at least four pounds.

## The Fall

1.

This is the season
of smoke

of syrupy wasps
crawling intoxicated,

the season of hot brick
a-blaze with vine, and I

spend my time swimming
loving my strength

led by a ruthless body
length after length

legs forked with sunlight
in poison-green water

kicking—
watch out!

2.

Being in this state—
that is not a free state

we circle the garden looking for a place to *be*
ashamed and vain in our nakedness

so we sit in the middle of everything
surrounded by chainsaws and bonfires

they are cutting down trees
and no one is stopping them.

Like drunken wasps, we
topple

into the smoke.
This is the season

of bird calls, bright grass
of camouflage

the sky seamless
we lie uncovered

under a sun that won't be turned off
as our bodies break open.

3.

This is the time of the purple moon
sinister, exceptional

a bloomed grape
a shard of silver, lemon sharp, oh

aren't we the decadents,
collapsing into the green pool

as the first leaves
crackle and spark

here, my arms,
the soft-shoe shuffle, the gentle guitar

and we are dancing, dancing
up here on the hill

while the city below us
burns.

## Green-eyed

Up here on the cliffs you see below
a swathe of lake, green
as a false jewel. Trick of light yet

the arbutus can only be a woman
and you see, you see, the classics persist,
a shape in the rock: shoulders, waist, hips.

Soon these woods will be a-chime with crimson.
After six years of duality, the
he/she balance that glides through the world
hiding all its tricks. You already want

to go back to that room—the one
with the four poster bed and the mirror.
You lean from the balcony, the hot hit
of cedar makes you gasp.

# Heron

—and in the morning
we are mannered and theatrical,
lounging like film stars in deck chairs with our
big-boned tea-cups, Judy Garland and me (who?),
grave in blue silk dressing gowns.

Around us, fennel
has grown careless, given up. The parched grass
gasps out its last, hot smell.
You, possessive through binoculars,
scan the ferries as they slide
sexily by.

All afternoon, a slow sun will pull shadow
inexorably over rocks. End of summer.
Soon you'll go. Already, dry leaves—so
beloved of poets and other compulsive nostalgics—
gather, irritable, on the deck.

A rude caw, and the heron—who has
also been posing since June—lurches
across the bay, prehistoric, unimpressed.
The vertebrae of rock where it had been, diminishing,
trickling into the sea.

# Fungi

On the fourth day it rained. Mushrooms
appeared easily on the lawn, egg-topped,
ash-white, and a solid burnish
came over the sea.

In the woods behind the house, fungi
took on a new sense of ownership and business;
logs were draped with vivid saddles, carrot-coloured
like a daring shirt, and the air in there
smelled of fresh-meal.

Down by the shore, a muddy odour, more brackish.
The gullies that yesterday
had faint tracings of streams feathered into their sand,
ran loud.

I wanted to sleep, the sea pearl, the sky
such thick, white gauze. But the woods
clamoured with cinnamon-brown scallops
that overlapped like shingles.
With stubby cups and creamy dinner plates,
their gilled undersides a lilac that suggested
wounding—or the fear of it.

# Aerial

## Landing

Flying low, pressing through the calm, wounded air,
we follow the big branch of river, jagged, blue

licks of shadow, swathe
of road and light.

The river
is a crack in pavement, a track
laid down to separate

this bruised, unfamiliar land, the
wrinkled mud flats: crusted with salt and tide.

Shoved, folded land, squeezed and elbowed,
the struggle for breath.

It is also          memory. Melancholy
for the Welsh hills, their
abandoned mines,

the bright lit years of childhood
that go on, seismic, unfolding and
unfolding. The river is both

its own strong spine,
and a scar badly stitched.

I can only speak of its shape,
though sometimes it floats                              rises up

into the haze like a water-snake
and we become  everything:          air          sea

until              Slam-land.
A cringing cheek, the rough hand
of arrival.

## Red Berry

From another plane window:
lichen, bark, moss.
       I have had these aerial views

too often lately, hazy and dislocated.
I have lived too much
on the hop. The toiling track of luggage, our pathetic—
and precious—
detritus.
       The red eye
of the automatic sink,
women's shoes under the toilet stalls, their sighs.

The fact is, I miss you.
I think of your teeth
as they bite along corn,
that dark cabin in the woods, a step forward, no more.
Your palm outstretched
as if testing for rain,
or begging.

       I have grown so wary.
Learnt a little
about the space between things.

For instance birch trees.
For instance, us,
this terrible fence-sitting.

The red berry in your palm has its own
dim power, a beautiful secret.
You hold it carefully,
loving its pulse, its
fear of you.

## Skating

We take our boys skating
and suddenly you're graceful. Swooping
away from me, your hands behind your back
in that easy pose.

A Prairie skill,
forced into your legs those early mornings
on the town hockey rink,
your father never doubting
he owned a son mean enough

to charge down other boys,
lock helmets, shove shoulders,
break teeth. So you learned
your country's basic language, enough
to leave it behind.

You circle me
as I inch with the toddlers, my hands
grasping air, my back's toppling arch.
*Lean forward*, you say, the ice
rasping under your blade
as you skid to a stop.

I'm awkward to your elegant
as you gently lead my four-year-old around the rink,
and I can't get enough of his face
as you return him to me,
flushed and beaming at the side of this man
that—by accident—I stumbled into
in this life.

## Skating in the Dark

My borrowed white skates teeter a path
over the rubbery floor, the damp
winter smell of small town hockey,
and, alone, I push off across the the empty rink.
Even in my body's bulky uncertainty
it is a sort of flying; my red mittened hands
reach for the gloom and somehow
my feet remember the push, the
strong swooping swim of it.

In the arena all is curtained, grey. Markers
that signify Canada's mysterious game
are like Kandinsky's stripes, red and blue
tracks, targets of blood
leaking under the ice.

I skate, and remember my mother.
Her headscarf tied under her chin, how she
braved London's violent, complicated suburbs
to take us skating. Then, that bad fall
when she chipped her knee and we didn't go again.

My irritation at her accidents,
of which I was one.
I don't know how I got here, to this
small prairie town, this empty hockey rink.
Nothing is how I planned it.

Thinking of her, I fall, hard, as if a hand
reached in to tangle my feet. She
bruised easily and I'll bruise too,
another purple continent
blooming under our white skin.

## The Fly

Wake with murderous impulses,
try to swat the fly with *Meadowlands*

and fail—those tiny black army vehicles
know I hate them.

I've been dreaming
of Saskatchewan roads, Roman straight.

Trying to make sense of it, how I
yearn for comfort yet

recoil from my lover's
orphaned greed. I am

my mother's daughter, her hands
knotted and stiff

from twisting flour and lard, and still
we gulp at her thick soup

as she rushes from room to room
balancing plates. I grew up

her ventriloquist's doll.
*Peas in a pod. Can't tell you two apart.* Yesterday

I took the canoe out again and the lake
mirrored cloud. Drifting over green

was to view like astronauts
the marbled earth below.

Believe me,
I am trying to make sense of it.

## The Forks

Today the city was on the turn, edging round
the corner into Spring.
You saw snowdrops,
their small appeal, their bravery.
And rooks in bare branches, nests
like clots in lungs—how can they
believe they're hidden?

You have forsaken Vancouver's golden forsythia.
Lonely, sure, but what kind of a woman
does not want that paired-up life?
Today you crossed the wooden foot bridge
with a sudden memory of desire;
strong, like the perfume of the wood.

You are on the turn.
You have stayed out late alone
with the people who sit
around the fire at The Forks,
tobacco smoke streaming from their mouths
like gentle dragons', the woodsmoke
smudging the air blue.

Someone told you about the river,
how it floods every year at this time.
Tonight it's swollen, sloshing, talking to itself.
You think of the flight attendant who told you
the worst part of the job
was being touched all the time.
On her days off she feels tender, bruised.

How would it be
to lie alongside her and not to touch?
To lie together on this hotel bed
staring back at
the voyeuristic moon?

## You Slip Into It

How hard it is to lose the self! And merge
even for a moment, with the wood, or the air,
or even to believe—for an instant
—that desire  can be more than a hunger
for an end to this chaffing loneliness. Without desire
there's relief, a vanilla scent in the room
and the candle's charred spool of smoke.

A long time ago you remember
sitting astride a wall—you were fifteen and slightly drunk,
so alight with lust only your skin held you in.

The forest is patient, the leaves won't hurt you,
they are turning yellow, the birch and poplar whisper
their serious game of hush.

This evening the lake was calm as you watched drops
pearl off the oar, rings opening and
opening. The khaki water was so flat it was
alive with reflection. You took photos
of the mirrored rushes and the boat drifted.
You lay on your back and looked at the sky
with which you were in love.

Your bed is narrow like a girl's. You must
love yourself because you are here, because in the winter
the lake freezes hard, but now the water is silky
against the tender warm spot on your back as you
slip into it and right now the lake
is orange tiger-striped. Tonight
you will dream of dark shapes pushing,
driving through the water—so much
remains unseen.

## A Week in an Abbey
## In the Middle of February

Everyone said, *you'll love it*. But I am, apparently,
unable to love. Yes, the room is full of snow-light,
generous mauve shadows ribbon the fields outside.
But this place smells of celibacy and old lunch. When
I was fourteen in Tunbridge Wells, *frigid* was the
word we most feared (floppy schoolgirl hair, shad-
owed eyes squinting into the sun, desire always, for
the wrong woman, the wrong man). When I walk
these corridors I am again that frightened girl, trip-
ping over my long feet, late for class, sanitary tow-
els and cigarettes in my bag, ink-stained, ashamed.
This place shrinks me. That sweet-rot pungency of
hair, beds, floor-polish. I turn a corner and expect
rebuke of a towering school-mistress. Portraits of
the glaring dead in their pie-crust bonnets, their
purple dresses, breasts packed solid as moors. Be-
tween that time and now: years. The miles. Seas of
snow. Surely I have come too far to find again these
polished corridors, this red-faced brick, these star-
tled prison windows? I cannot pray for forgiveness,
I do not believe in sin.

## Yoga Journal

*Day One*

Breathe
       my busy mind
that fiddles and frets
with driving and paychecks and
TV and lunch and the comfort of

trance. That's the trick of it.

Like the woman who could
hold her breath underwater for
six and a half minutes

       breathe,

beloved body
where have you been,

when now skin speaks
only loss
and it's been years now
of kissing a dead man,

knowing it's hopeless.
Why pretend?

Though everyone pretends, more or less,
touches life with gloves on.


When I arrived last night
the pipes had burst, all the cisterns
overflowing and a woman with a mop.

Good sign. Waters breaking,
the overflow and gush, I
wanted that,

to stumble
in deep snow, can't tell
when you'll walk upright like you
own the place, or

be swallowed, cut off at the knees
and it's all recovery
and struggle—

and always the white,
its extravagant drifts and waves, land's
genius.

Breathe.

*Day Two*

Body's fragile uncertainty.

Through the wall I can hear
the monks singing

and me, wobbling in tree-pose

can't quite—

yet—

morning light pours itself slowly, slowly
over the fields and on the wall

a Celtic cross of shadow
balances superbly

*Day Three*

Last night I dreamt you'd finally died.
I woke swaddled and airless,
swimming out of sleep as if through
deep snow, remembering

those terrible evenings
ruined by drinking and darkness,
the violence of the talk
between women and men.

> *We speak, we utter words,*
> *but only later*
> *sense their life.*

*Day Four*

Beauty!
outside, petrified birch trees lacy w/hoar frost
cast their slim mauve shadows,

arterial

exhibitionist,
prettified,
off-to-the prom
off-the-rails

let's all go!
I'll wear lace too—so what
if gender is grief's mime-show

I do still have that small envelope
you seem to want so badly—

though these days
you're more like a maypole
with girls dancing
their complicated ribbons

and crabapples, just the size
of your mouth, so
red, a marvelous wheelbarrow full—

> *The beginning of day's brightening!*

I would love to be able to say that.
Hold the pose, a brave line, a hopeful line, so long, so
limber.

*Day Five*

The hall is dark, still.
The morning: skeletal.

Open.
Close.
Open.
Over flow; unfold, smudge

those thin bones of light, Sylvia's relics, drawn-out lines—
poetry
with its infinite possibility and
spray-on form—

though the inverse
is just as true. Steady

on strong long limbs. Both sides for balance. Both sides.

Body, gift-basket, unreliable nurse.
Touch my hot forehead, hold back my hair

I don't want perfection, that anorexic notion
nourished as it is by            *no*

Yes.
Last night the sky
was rich with stars, sieved light

Spruce assembled, bowed together
like praying monks

and snow blew, wraith-like, shimmying
low on the fields.

*Day Six*

The sky finally lightening, morning. Mourning,
it takes so long.  In thick syrup
I have preserved you. Still

waiting
for the world to bring me
long stemmed roses, a shy delivery. Their light
weight, a

> *gentle*
> *exploration, touching*
> *pen to paper in that spirit of inquiry*

follow the trail
of blue ribbons tied on the branches,

last night's dream dissolving like desire, like pain.

Spirit. Cupped hands. All the women's footprints
in the snow that make it easier

to breathe.

*St. Peter's Abbey, Sask.*

# Call

I sit in this snow-lit room,
cheating on the family again with poetry,
my little scratch-scratch.
I could stop and do the dishes, or
I could go search half-heartedly
for my heart, which—I'm guessing—
is buried somewhere out there,
under snow's thick white medicine.

It's buried, lost, and it may
be gone some time. I call for it
like a woman in a house coat
coaxing in a cat, she's holding a cigarette
and has had a drink or two.
She hates the snow. It piles up
bright around her door.
*Heart! Heart!* she whispers (she
doesn't want the neighbours to hear),
*Are you there?*

Thaw

the soft chant
of water rushing far away
the hush      of ash

there is a word
for the single flaw
that makes the elegant whole

but look around, furrows
of dark earth emerge from snow
like the first lands      cracking a white sea

there is sun on the thaw

the small
neat slippers of animal tracks
thread their necklace      off
into the woods

a fence throws sharp purple lines
and the softer lattice of trees

more vague
more blue

and hush      stand still

Nuthatch
will flit down and feed
from your outstretched hand

Touch

My old father sits like Mattisse
in his lush garden, doves perched upon his hand.
Remember the dangers he told us about?
The knife wounds, the dog bites, the ruinous dives
into shallow pools?
Firework burns, champagne corks,
boat propellors, a choking
dressing gown cord. His patients' accidents
got his attention.

I touch the spice box on the mantle,
the fire spitting and wind in the chimney.
Touch it all, a postcard from Vienna,
the embossed invitations: "At Home",
the silver matchbox with its seal—
a lion for silver, a leopard's head for London.
I feel their Braille.

Remember the sweet smell of his soap,
of whisky, or sherry if it was noon, his heathery
tweed jacket, my grip on his lapel.
But what empty shape would all that clutter
fill now I am so foreign
from that child with her longings
like dark shameful moss?

He is a grandfather clock that has stopped ticking.
No one loves in the right way. Can tell
the difference between a wound and a cut,
the line between accident and purpose
too fine, almost impossible
to read.

## Again, the Prairie

—as if this time, the naked fields might confess,
or the long line of spruce with their glittering
glass rims of salt and the train tracks' true blue taper—

because the eye
seeks boundary, order.

At first there is silence, darkness. No voice.
Why do you choose to suffer?
Incessant pills of snow sift through the air.
No cell phone          you are out of range. No radio signal
but an anxious, warning hiss.

You were not born for this. You have always
gone too far, stretched thin the miles
till nothing and no one could reach you.

This elongated winter has ground on
for too long, contentment has been refused
like food or the delicate wrought-iron chair
you prefer to leave tipped over, with its
small burden of snow.

For years you have been a child in the dark, searching
for clues, believing you were not wanted but
if you were good you might be safe. And the inverse of that.

So you preserve. Loss,     ice.     A robin's egg-
shell blue hut in the woods where you might
hoard, gather. Brother. Lover. White
tablet on my tongue, I am trying to let you go.

The message is buried here somewhere, encoded, engraved.
Little light, I know you

are all the more fragile
under the weight I insist you bear.

## Bone Song

The bone-doctor's embrace
unlocks a hidden cracking song.

Naked branches. I want you like water.
Birds: my clavicles, silver birds or

real birds, sipping at a bowl of rain
sipping at my empty clavicles

brittle wingspan stuck
in this separation, this salty-cellar.

I would share my silver birds with you,
calm on the mantle.

Close the window, hush
the banging of the wind out there.

## What We Don't Do

Today I bought a silver ring, hoping its sky-blue
stone might carry a part of you with me.
Leaving, such sad surgery. I read somewhere
that words are only recognised
after they're uttered. Why speak?

The birds in the winter trees
let go their fountain of song, bold and furious,
a shaking-out of their small lives.
But I'm silent, I'm shy with you.

When we met, my fingertips
recognised your mouth, or wanted to.
Weighing that careful balance
between acting, then what? They say it's
what you don't do you regret.

Let's gather up one of the white pillows
that sit plump in the fulcrum of trees,
bring a blanket too. We'll
walk in the woods, falling in and
falling in. Let's stay, until the sky
writes us into spring. Your eyes are very blue.
Here, on my finger, a ring.

# Mars

I am planning a day in the future, a dark red room.
Ask and it shall be given. I know

that to try and climb a childhood tree again
is to crash through dry old branches,

roots below like swimmer's arms
caught mid-stroke.

Tonight, Mars is a dim carnation in the sky.
The frosty lawn of Northern lights

and the moon jealous, blood-orange too.
It's the forest fires make it that way,

earthly, you can smell them,
and last night there were ashes in the pool.

What can it be to lose everything?

Non-attachment,
non-attachment.

We do not say Grace, but
wish it were so.

## The Empress

*. . . so that death*
*when it came,*
*wouldn't seem like a significant change*

Louise Gluck

## Sarsen

If I were to write you a poem I would
have to mention the Thames, its sombre brow
furrowed in thought. Because the icons
of the London skyline have changed
in the decade since I've been gone,
secrets and puzzles lie
under the beer-brown water
but it's tidal and sometimes
our eyes open to what's obvious
then close again. I wanted to tell you
about my blundering around the boulders
at Avebury, those Sarsen stones
like worn down chess pieces
surrounded by the gentle raise of the hills,
my mother's red scarf flowing behind her,
queenly. Boisterous clouds, rain and sun
shifting like temper. Let me tell you
not of water's dark closing
but about return. How nothing's lost.
the leash of place pulling at us,
then letting loose again.

## Girls and Boys

You want to swim naked again
through prehistoric summers
run through snaking tunnels
     of rhododendron, maze
of thick branch        root and sunlight

a swimming pool
and the warm brick wall      dreaming statue
dips her toe day and night
into the jewel blue

where children offer up their skulls
earning silver for doggy-paddles
and later
     lengths, underwater, the
blessed seal of silence.

High above you, pink roses drip
over the wall. A wrought iron gate.

Boys. Danger, of course. Always lurking,
powerful and mean, occasional kindness
(your name in charcoal
     writings' soft rasping breath)

Panting breath      tunnels      tunnels
of legs you had to crawl through  quick
they could hit you
hard as they like     that was the game

the bright cruelty          cheerful and
difficult to remember                    your doll
thrown quick into fire, stuffed rabbit's
neck hinged with open stitches     you knew

it was that absent part of you they hated,
the shut line
drawn down there,
like the arrowheads they hunted for
in the quarry.

## The Quarry

Like the blind girl in that Wyeth painting
she used to clamber here, listen
to the rustling gossip between aspen and wind.
She would fly a kite—imagined herself lifted,
drifting up and over the North Downs.
It was all grass then, and waving corn.
The hills a solid tidal wave, poised
to break. And full of money.

They dug, sucked out the valuable red sand,
the work was ruthless. But sometimes
she's glad; the quarry is a mess and she likes it.
A gulping bowl, its tossed sweep of cloud,
the few remaining trees straining and keening.
And she likes the tough little plants
that grew back, the thistle and poppy that
elbowed their way between the stones,
the fossils' filigree, the new moonscape
of cracked earth.

She has let silver-steel kites carry her
miles beyond the Downs, beyond England.
They can have the hills, the bright blonde fields.
Slap a motorway through. They can have
all those years that are over and dig them up.
But these they cannot have:
The yellow gorse that smells of coconut.
The fossil. The feather with its blue-black quill.
These she claims as she crouches
in the quarry's ruined amphitheatre,
hands on her knees, her eyes following
the hawk's free-wheel.

## Since I Got Back (a postcard)

It's all gone
quite well considering. Despite that bewildering in-
terface between friendship and lust, the troubling
dreams where sapphires spring from my ring and lit-
ter the floor trying to find you. Changing the "you"
to "one"and back again—trying to dumb it down.
Language remains a problem, an obstacle, but ex-
ile is like that. Truthfully, I'm in a kind of narcosis
here; the famous view of the mountain's bumpy
heart-monitor, sun funneling through cloud and a
spill of coins off the birch tree. Pristine quiet.
It sends me.

## Beth

This one's for Beth, gentle heiress who gave it all away.
Took the train to Amsterdam, set up in an empty hotel
overlooking the park: *The Hotel Amber*, its vines
and pillars and silence.

The night I found my way to her
I flipped up my cigarette lighter, the little flame
threading a path along dark corridors to the top floor,
a gold line of candlelight under a door,
and the room shrugging with shadow, spicy with hash, and

Lady Elizabeth, lying in repose, a yellow splinter
dancing in each black eye.
She worked cleaning offices, in the afternoons
joined jugglers in the park.
It was November, and cold. We ate
herring and onions from street vendors,
fries with mayonnaise.

Beth's hair was cropped, her ears and lip laddered, skewered
with silver fretwork. Climbing her pale arms:
tattoos like black lace gloves.
What's to say? We were twenty, we lost touch.
Were never *in* touch,

equal parts intimacy and distance, that exhausting balancing act
that cancels itself out. But Beth, I think of you,
your long fingers weaving the air, blur of ruby, smoke
of my amazed breath.

# Rainbow Party

The girl, her young mouth
wide open   O
closing over
it
starts to move back and forth
her lips' seal
and the warm
soft world
of tongue.

The boy closes his eyes—

it's

public          intimate          wordless          language
it's a plugging          a draining          a wetness          a power

a con          mystery          tradition          it's
gratitude          an exhange          a violence
castration          a stopping-up
an opening-up          a salve          binge          purge
a skill          a sport          a feeding          an incorporation
          communion          comfort

it's head          it's brain          it's biting          it's
bolus          it's threatening          envy          medical
silencing
          it's swallow          tongue          tidal
breath
shuddering          rapture          rupture          it's
theft

it's male
    it's a globe             it's a tunnel    a longing
    a metaphor           it's Sapphic    kneeling
    theatre      gossip        a sedative
    it's milk     hair   heat        it's neck
    it's drowning
O
it's circular          homework          history
basements
    acne    oysters       routine      transgressive
    it's phallic        it's
                                        not

# Halifax

Easing the white meat from the lobster
(can't speak of *eating flesh*), she
thinks about the boiling water,
hopes it was quick, hopes it was
worth it. Everyday the hotel corridor
smells of fish. This city
is a museum of fire and drowning.

Sheets wrapped around
the gift of her white shoulders
she thinks, *wound*, thinks, *rape*.
A pull-out couch, white
panties on the floor and a TV cheering
from the room next door.

She runs the bath, scalding, washes and
washes away the thick smell of sea
(the lost girl, a smashed cake).
Some things are still too dangerous.

She wishes she could go back
to that young, hard, cinema-mind
she used to wrap herself in; such ideas
saved her, protected
underneath, the dark delicacy.

## The Stone

Remembering the girl—the one
we all called slut but also copied,
her silver eye make-up, her coat
with the faux-fur collar.
She told me once of
being fucked in the woods,
a stone lodged under her spine,
and the boy thrust harder
thinking her cries meant pleasure.
Remembering that story
(the branches
a silvery puzzle above
me, the stone).

## The Trees

I walked up the stone steps to the white house
with its Italianate arched windows. Snow
was beginning to fall and as I climbed
I was aware of leaving myself behind,
lightly shedding any wisdom or discernment
I may have learned, as I would later shed my clothes,

a soft trail from room to room, the glass of champagne
tipping wetly in my hand. The man, quiet and
baffling to me, with his tie collection, his
sprawling open suitcase of clothes, dusty paintings
casually stacked against the walls. Even
the surprise of the warm animal between us
could not flower him. All night

I watched the winter trees outside the window,
their dark filigree spread out over the sky
as it slowly rolled toward dawn. I was afraid
of what I recognised there, my greed and longing
for flowers I had once held my face to
in another country, their sweet fragrance
I had thought lost.

# La Source

Far reaching. Profligate really, this yellow.
And August, most dissolute of months!

Barely contained in its floral dress it
spills quietly, overblown and hopeless.

Smoking. A woman of a certain age,
but the French love that. Lizards. A fan.

Shutters banging at the top of the house
a strange early morning wind, ill,

portentous, before the sun takes over.
Broody wasps slow-picking

their doomed embroidery
in the wine glass you left out last night,

flies insist in the dark kitchen,
white light behind shutters, white light and

a plane tree, its leopard skin bark, go,
run your hands over it.

**French Still Life**
**(With Lemons And Nectarines)**


This house used to be a silk-worm mill, now
it's a holiday home. Not the whirr

of looms but the
splash and cry of privileged children

around a swimming pool
veiled by vineyards. A tray of nectarines—

*don't eat them, I might want to paint them*
My red dress

stretched out to dry in the sun.
Butterflies and lemon trees,

lizards, their flickering tails.
Your unlikely wife

with her nose-ring and her
purple trousers.

And acres of sunflowers—
their dumb, happy faces

—turned.

**Balcony**

Squinting into opera glasses my
belief in the pure relationship

between the eye and
Carmen in her black dress a

red carnation in her hair
I become another

contamination, like a man
erasing her, arousing

something foreign
in my eye

## A Toast

The dark restaurant,
its heavy velvet drapes,

a shared cigarette, the edge
of a glass, the edge

of your beautiful mouth.
We drink without irony

to *happiness*, places
we'd like to visit some day,

money, success, travel.
All vapourous

as the taste of gin
in our mouths.

Tea-lights glimmer on the tables
like tiny campfires

far below a plane window.
The world

of crumbs you gather
with the edge of your hand.

Let's go.

## The Pull

Artifice,
that is to say: paint. Loving that,
how rough and smudged it is,
how she allows
so much
to show through.

      Artful, her
broken camouflage.

That is to say,
her broken history, her
smudged mouth, cheek,

cashmere,
old fur. All that
         potent burlesque
that men        claim
to want (lace, paint).

      Of course,
mostly it is the mother-pull, nostalgia
(yes, comfort, warm perfume, all that).

But it is also
her hands.
How strong they are,
chipped and accomplished, her
naked feet.

Desire.
It is always the same.
Its folly.
Its stubborn inability to
live in contentment.

Underground streams—the source:
a red, wet mouth.

**After Yoga**

Lying on my back next to my new friend
looking up together at the cherry blossom, she is
framing it with her hands.

Yoga, the very word.

Curled in child-pose and remembering—
but that was so long ago, a dream, and we are all
only children in our imaginary worlds.

Surely
this is happiness, walking down the street after yoga
carrying yellow tulips, your arms too
overflowing with flowers and we are talking
about poetry, the streets piled high
with ticker-tape magnolia, cherry and here
we have found spring.

# Vancouver, June

Griping about wanting a better car, where's
the poetry in that? Your friend mentions
she's leaving to live out east; her little
hard-earned daughter sits, softly imitating crows.

A massive pink cloud, solid and slow
makes its thoughtful procession between
the high-rises at Denman, this city
shocking in its summer reveal, when clouds

like leisurely spaceships arrive at sunset
unnerving us again to dumb awe, almost love.
The crows swerve apart; you brush
clinging pollen off your shoulder
as a flowering tree crumbles a little.

## Walk

Birds scatter like cinder, scared
by their own echoes, the past
circling back at them, urgent.
You wipe cobwebs from your face
like tears, your throat aching with them.
You are grateful. A table of women

speaking of their mothers' deaths;
now we know more, we are
more tender. Soft twig,
grass and tinder under naked feet,
the deer at the side of the road
a skein of white rope

pouring from its haunch—
you can't look. All animals
are afraid, skitter from air
and you, afraid,
like a child in the dark, of headlights
blazing down the hill, black shape
at the wheel.

## The Empress

Naked
on an unmade bed          a mermaid on a rock
          she can hear       the seagulls throaty cry     dumb and erotic
and all around    the deep boom of the hotel,
its heart-
beat.

She's floating on the bed, an island
in this chintz room she hired,
          each room
a cell in the hive.

No one knows she's here
          it's like a death          an erasure          (she
stays away from the window
          believes in the pull          in sudden helplessness)

          The hotel
is dressed in ivy and ivory,
a desiccated tiger
rears over the fireplace, snarling and flattened.

The ping          of the elevator, the surprise of it
opening          and who
might be standing there.          She is

          a woman          toppling into middle age,
she is          the fat lady in the mirror
resigned to the fuggish clan of her body
          its ordinary secrets  ·

she is            eating birthday cake (a small silver fork)
her brain's intestines    closely packed        a knot
of thought      a flock of naught

flock vines climb the walls.        She wonders
                    if she has been greedy,
like the British Museum, collected more
than she needed—

past lovers swarm        like military elite, like ground-cover.
Sometimes
she'd like to return all the artifacts, all the relics.

            One true thing:
*la jouissance*—the mother-bliss.
She has known that
            (and what I say is the truth so help me God).

Along *The Shining* corridors
hang sepia photographs:
                    big ships        plough their way into this land.

Beyond velvet drapes            pink flowers
read:            *Welcome to Victoria.*

Up close they're
flowers,            up close she
is mired
a        mother, her smothering skirts
(*mere            mer*            the sea
                                of the body).

Up close she is cranky w/frown lines,
vain and depressive        she is

82

forty          cosseted by heredity          eating cake
          secrets   fizzing in her blue veins
in her wrists                    her shaking hands

Winds are calm. Seas are rippled.
          Today
happiness is tended silence,
the hotel room's isolation tank          a port
neither here
                         nor there

The small ship of cake is a pretty thing,
its strata of red gel, its snowy glaze

She is not (at heart) a *femme*, her elegance
          imported, Miss-Fit,
but she can't help
her hugely soft, female body

and she has always
          loved lilies          their thick scent, their staining hearts,

          all the interior spaces
of femininity:

the parlours          the dining rooms          the gardens
she ponders them
          in her heart

The past streams out behind her
its terrible flare,
Isadora's scarf          tangled in the spokes.

In this new country
she loves the log booms    those gatherings
of past lives
jostling and waiting,
        how they
hitch together              how they
unhook.


But still          she is hostage to Wordsworth, the chiffon mist,
the cold sweat of dew

to the dark topiary at Hever, the carp
that slowly patrol the moats.

Nostos isn't cricket—that dreary paradigm of death,
isn't      teashops          tins of tea, Harrods    Christ! all that.

It's the gestures    the hats
frozen in the air: good bye
good bye          I'm gone          I'm gone          I'm gone
I'm gone          I'm

it's the white iris bulbs she brought over, wrapped in muslin
struggled to re-plant        (pathetic
trying to re-create Sissinghurst
in a six-foot-square balcony). That narrative

embarrasses her now.  Her privileged story of loss
seems juvenile              sentimental,  yet
        it's the balm that makes sense, gives reason
to fetish,          fetish
to egress, to the
pink ribbon round the love letters
the photographs
the pressed flowers

those small ruins          where memory stays
where happiness is dust, is a
bouquet          a necklace          a thrown hat.

          Love,
spread thick, its lovely
glaze.

Silver Collection

## Silver Collection

### 1/

*Inkstand—double Chester Edwardian, round w/ pen holes, late Victorian*

—pencil softly in the shadow, the silvery
sheen around his eyes.
He was always—      (wrong
     to say: white, like the pages of a book, wrong
     to say: ivory)

a quiet boy, soft blonde cuttings of hair
lying on the floor around his chair.

He was soft,
*say it:* bent (the ink
of society's newspapers
tarnishing his hands)


on the wall, a shivering square of light,
a water-mark

### 2/
     *Sarah has taken a clock worth I guess about forty pounds*
     *and David a cigarette case.*

     I'm keen on the pair of small birds (Asprey's 1905)
     but I bet I'm not the only one

Between us: the miles.
And all we are
is soft, living      malleable—
our warm skin, inner ear a pearly shell—

not towering creatures with leopards' heads,
not lions.

> *Nostalgia*
> *is not a longing for a place*
> *but for time—*
> *childhood, or*
> *the slower rhythm of dreams*

—*6 George III "Bright Cut" (feathered) tablespoons with rampant lion*
    *crest*
—*12 Victorian dessert forks (Edinburgh) fiddle pattern handle with*
    *scallop*
—*Pair sauce ladles with strange crest*
—*6 teaspoons Victorian, unreadable crest*

Hey, diddle diddle
The cat and the fiddle—

You've got to watch her
or she'll take the lot, and you'll end up
with the bronze—

> *Christening mug by Charles Thomas Fox & George Fox*
> *1848, 8 sided Teething Spoon*

Whatever happened to Baby Jane?
She grew up    put on a hat
rode a silver kite across the sky,
looked down at mountains, all bunched
gully and snow-trickle, then
smooth
white plains. Firm and simple
(not at all like the pages of a book)

wanting
to lie down in that deep snow, in love, like Gerald
*how frail the thread of his being was stretched!*

> *if you keep looking back it will*
> *paralyze you, turn you*
> *into a monument*
> *to your own grief*

Saskatchewan? Wear the Fox Hat?

3/

> *Tea set, including tea pot, sugar bowl w/ 2 handles, milk jug.*
> *Goldsmith and Silversmith Co. 1904. Well used.*

Remember those Decembers?
*a million tapers flaring bright from twisted silvers*
the gins and tonics, the silver-fizz,
and *the silver doctor, also a very great favourite*
*tag, tinsel,*
*tail, a topping; but turn*
*of red crewel, a body*
*of silver tinsel entirely—*

> *sugar bowl 1905   17th C style, ornate*

A five layer cake
garnished with roses
white scalloped ribbons, a web of
hard spun sugar. We were all
gently hammered
and his eyes
were a bright silver-ish blue

## 4/

*N'gland* is a *merde-haus* (sick).
At night
the curtains are left open, the sky
tragic w/ charcoal clouds

Burglars from Bromley or Sidcup
snoop in the homeless dark,
magpies, scoping out the silver carriage clock,
the writing desk,
the white-flecked sea-scape.
*Everything: an absence.*

Come and get it boys.

Or, me, a peep show
curled in my mother's chair
watching Reality on the telly (glued, let's face it),

it's got down to five of them now, locked in a house together

> *You are at once homesick and*
> *sick of home.*
>    *Mustard Pots:*
> *—small watering can with green lining and mirror in lid*
> *—Georgian pot like a barrel w/blue glass lining*

*Speak roughly to your little boy,*
       *And beat him when he sneezes:*
*He only does it to annoy,*
       *Because he knows it teases*

> *—Pepper pot shaped like an acorn, about 2 inches high. V.*
> *dented, but sweet, probably late Victorian*

These are things that make me nervous:

my dad
standing to pee with the door open,
his shoulders raised, head bowed.
The loud flush.

A phone's
tremulous ringing, its thin, warning cry—

the arrogant *thwack* and call of Wimbledon
living room's murky olive light, curtains drawn at noon—
a school of fish might easily drift on
through the French windows

> *Collection of odd spoons:*
> > *jam spoon, scallop shape*
> > *sugar tongs, 2*
> > > *1 large ornate mustard spoon (or, I suppose jam or relish!)*

The click of knitting needles
and a toilet's flush

> *Porringer—copy of a Georgian design; twin handled,*
> *about 4 inches across and high*

While we sleep, the barns
are pyres.
In the morning there'll be
a photo of a lamb on the front page of *The Telegraph*,
the farmer raising it up like a prize, the beige curls at its throat,
cloven feet bleakly pedaling—

*there is a sort of solitude that*
*touches every traveler leaving home,*
*a melancholy*
*that lives deep within the excitement*
*or any purpose*
*that might prompt the journey*

*4-legged salt dish, Geo III, claw feet, good gauge, sturdy*

My mother shakes her head as we drink gin and tonics
and watch the evening news together.
*It's terrible,* she says,
*those poor creatures.*
*And the worst of it*
*is the landscape now—so*
*empty, so barren . . .*

She tosses cubes of floured cow into a frying pan, it
sizzles and shrinks.
*A beautiful bit of beef that, Mrs. Pearson, silverside.*

5/
        *Jugs:*
*—small milk, 1888, half-fluted, good gauge (i.e. weight) and condition*
*—small milk, Georgian, plain*

Jane grows up
and forgets
how once she fed greedily
upon those breasts
        (silver-sitting in the dark
        the sky across the valley
        blooming china-blue)

Language
gathering, lining up in her mouth,
blurred sounds tapping at the icy window.
 *Listen*, her small fingers
mark the air—

> *teaspoon lightly engraved with initials AP (shd. go to Adam)*
> *2 pushers (for babies)*

> > *You know it is a*
> > *tantalizing romance,*
> > *an unaffordable luxury.*

> *Candlestick—probably Sheffield plate; rather battered.*

6/

Jane,
are you still up there in the attic, sitting in the dark?
what are you *doing* up there?

> > *A hypochondria of the heart*
> > *that thrives on its own symptoms—*

(tarnished, hollow
under absolute   neglect)

> *wine-coaster, fretted with 2 handles and 4 stubby legs.*
> *Fairly useless for a bottle so big,*
> *but you might stand a plant on it.*
> *Not worth the cleaning if you ask me*

> We had terrible smog that year, a real pea-souper.
> I knew I was on Regent Street but had no idea where—
> then, I remember, I reached out my hand
> and touched          Liberty

95

*—nostalgic love is rarely reciprocated,*
*and if your choice was fitting at the time,*
*spare yourself the guilt.*

Tooth-marks.
Water-marks.
Water-babies.

Stains
that remain.
Remains
that bleed and blossom
all over the page.

(—a cold day, Trafalgar Square,
lines of women chanting:
*Free abortion on demand!*

Spectres of statues
black against October clouds)

My mother's soft belly, her stretch marks
a shoal of minnows trailing—

*fish knives and forks, set of 6 each. Danish silver with bone handles.*
*(not dishwasher friendly)*

What if the silver-blue cord                *is* the only reason to love?
(Oh guilt! Spare me)

Chatelaine—with gilt. Value to be confirmed

*The home-coming did not cure her at all,*
*only aggravated the longing*

Ladybird, ladybird.
Won't you come home?
Rivers of gin are
streaming from your eyes

      *salts—a pair of small birds, 1905 (Aspreys)*

71

      *My aspens dear*
             the soft of water
     rushing far away

the hush
    of ash

      there is a word
                for the single flaw
                that makes the elegant whole

      but look       the silver birch
      its bright grey skin, its

Japanese negative space

how through broken trees
     new ones push—

(and shh
            stand still

     nuthatch
     will flit down
     and feed
     from your outstretched palm)

*a set of 4 boat shaped-salts with blue glass linings,1805*

I am lonely without you.
All the things I said I'd never be,
I am.

**8/**

> *Vase, filigree, lined with blue glass, early 20th C*
> *Bon-bon dishes, 3 scalloped, i.e. like a scallop shell and that size.*
> *Probably Edwardian*

The sky and the land probably *did* meet,
but there was no way of verifying it—

pearl was all, pearl—
or, was it more opal
    and the faintest *ghost* of a pink?

Top hat and tails, the *glamour* of snow back then!
art-deco shadows that laced the lawn
                     crystalline
                            *silver-silent*
(buried silver
buried bone)

**9/**

The silver-band in their scarlet jackets
played *California Here We Come*
(every cloud has a charcoal lining)

red poppies blow        a kiss—
*and the dish ran away with the spoon*

        *bon-bon dish, art dec. A swirling leaf*

98

—silver needles of rain pierce the puddles, mud
furrowed for planting
bodies.    *What grew?*

*6 apostle-headed tea-spoons in a case. Undistinguished but useful.*

Barbed wire.
Poppies. Snowdrops,
their frail necks, their bravery
(memories sickly
          pastoral hum)

—and the snow continues to fall
like some kind of          wisdom

**10/**

A wedding bouquet of lilies
my grandmother in her pearls,
her shining ivory silk     *touches the future*
                           *like silver, like a blade—*

how our hands
are like birds
when bad news hits,
how they fly
to block our mouths, or
clap together in useless prayer—

        *tea-pot. Victorian, small, round, lightly engraved. "Bullet" shaped.*

One for sorrow, two for joy—

A swirling leaf—
quick!  Run across the bridge
        and wait for it—

*wanders the hoary Thames along his silver winding way—*

Her milky cataracts
watching the grey
smoke rising from her tea—Lapsang Souchong.

She wears her cherished brooch of grief.
It keeps. It does not age.

The click of knitting needles.
Smoke.
Dominoes.
Magpies.
The collapsing bodies
        of books

*—and through the long-nailed fingers glide*
*the silver-shining minnows (a list of absences)*
*on you glide, till you reach the summit-edge,*
        *then over*

# Notes and Acknowledgments

Earlier versions of some of these poems have appeared in the following literary journals: *Prism International, The Capilano Review, Arc, Grain, CV2, Event*. And in the anthologies *Listening with the Ear of the Heart*, eds: Dave Margoshes and Shelley Sopher (St.Peter's Press 2003); *To Find Us, Words and Images of Halifax*, ed. Sue Macloud, 2005; *Contemporary Northwest Poets*, ed. David Biespiel.

Silver Collection was first published in an art catalogue to accompany Mary Kavanagh's exhibition polish, August 23th-October 5th 2003, organised by the Medicine Hat Museum and Art Gallery, Alberta. Thank you Mary, and thanks to Betsy Warland for facilitating this rewarding collaboration.

Quotes in *Yoga Journal* are from the sources indicated: Aurora by Sharon Thesen, *Aurora*, Coach House Press 1995; When Angels Leave by Robyn Sarah, *Questions About The Stars*, Brick Books 1998.

Silver Collection incorporates text from: *The Future of Nostalgia* by Svetlana Boym (Basic Books 2001). It also quotes from: *The Tempest* and *Richard 11*, William Shakespeare; *Roman Balcony*, David Gascoyne; Ode On A Distant Prospect of Eton College, Thomas Gray; Some of the Women, Erin Moure from *Domestic Fuel*, Anansi; *Women In Love*, D.H.Lawrence; *Ulysses*, James Joyce; *The Bible, Eccl. X11; Alice's Adventures In Wonderland*, Lewis Carroll; *The Poetical Works of Robert Browning; Binsey Poplars*, Gerard Manley Hopkins. Above all, Silver Collection is indebted to Robert Kroetsch's poem Seed Catalogue, upon which it is loosly based. Thanks to Robert Kroetsch and Betsy Warland for their generous readings of Silver Collection, and special thanks to Rosemary Pearson for the original archival list.

Here I am, Lover is for Mark Cochrane; After Yoga is for Esta Spalding; Heron is for Angela Grossmann; Green-Eyed is for Tanis Macdonald; Boys and Girls is for Dill Anstey; Fungi is for Michael Pearson;

Sarsen is for Rosemary Pearson; Silver Collection is for Sarah Gull and David Pearson.

I wish to extend appreciation to the following people: Mark Cochrane, Daphne Marlatt, Aislinn Hunter, Roo Borson and Michael Carroll for their helpful reading of some of these poems, and particular thanks to Barry Dempster for his tactful and incisive editorial hand on this manuscript, and his kindness.

The Saskatchewan Writer's Guild and all at Emma and Christopher Lakes and at St. Peter's Abbey where many of these poems were written. Esta Spalding for the Bowen cabin. The Currie Family for introducing me to Hornby Island. Stephen Raycraft. Hiro Boga and Ron Smith at Oolichan for catching this book when it was free-falling. My father Michael Pearson for his photograph, "Tatsfield, 1963". And of course much gratitude to the Canada Council and the Arts Council of British Columbia for their generous financial support.

Author photo by Adrienne Theissen, Gemini Visuals

Miranda Pearson was born in England and came to Canada in 1991 to work as a psychiatric nurse. She is a graduate of the University of British Columbia's MFA program in Creative Writing, where she was also on faculty. Miranda is currently the poetry "mentor" at Simon Fraser University's Writer's Studio. Her poetry has been published widely in literary journals and anthologies. *The Aviary*, her second book of poetry, is the winner of the Alfred G. Bailey Prize 2006, awarded by the Writer's Federation of New Brunswick.